Annie's Ark

Lesley Harker

The Chicken House

It's raining again and Grandaddy Noah says,
"Annie, little Annie, come and feed the llamas.
They're making such a clatter with their hooves again."

So I get up from my corner, my nice dry corner,
where the wind doesn't blow and the drips don't drip.

First I feed the llamas, and then I groom the antelope.

When they settle down, I rock the lambs to sleep.

I rock this way and I rock that way, and the water keeps squelching in my hobnail boots.

Now Mother is calling, "Annie, little Annie,
the chickens are loose in the larder again."

So I run and I clap, I chase and I chivvy,
and everyone's flapping and clucking at me.

Uncle Shem is shouting, "Help me, little Annie, I'm stuck in the stairway. I'm tripping over penguins and the monkeys are climbing all over me."

I run and I flap and I shoo them away, and the water keeps sloshing in my hobnail boots.

I'm looking for a corner, a nice quiet corner, to think about sunshine and bright blue skies.

But the corners are crowded - even the wettest - with lions and tigers and big black bears.

Now Grandma is calling, "Annie, little Annie.
Come now quick - fetch these snakes away!
They're tangling up my knitting and knotting up my wool.
Annie, little Annie, please rescue me."

So I push them and pull them and wind them up neatly,
and the water keeps sploshing in my hobnail boots.

I'm going to try hiding, way up high -
where no one can see me at all.
I'm getting so cosy, everything's peaceful . . .

till Grandaddy Noah comes
looking for me.
He's shouting up the ladder,
"Is the water still rising?
Are the waves still tossing on
the wild, wild sea?"

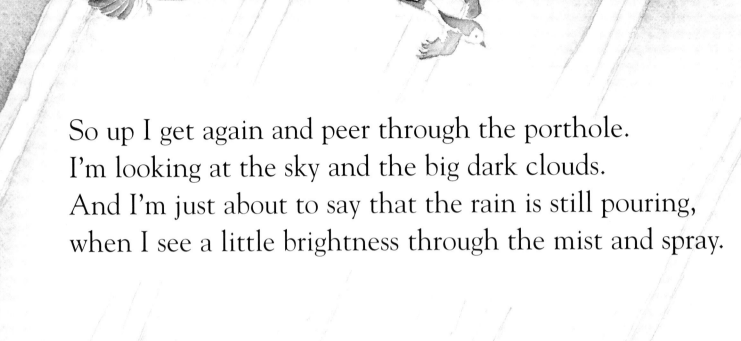

So up I get again and peer through the porthole.
I'm looking at the sky and the big dark clouds.
And I'm just about to say that the rain is still pouring,
when I see a little brightness through the mist and spray.

"Grandaddy, Grandma, Mamma and Papa!
Uncles and aunts and animals too!

Come here everyone,
everybody *QUICK* now."

Grandaddy Noah called for a dove
and sent it to search
for some life in the brightness.
And it went and it looked and it found
a leaf. And everybody said . . .

Then Grandaddy Noah said, "Come quick little Annie, clever little Annie, dear little Annie!"

And everyone laughed and everyone cried,
and we danced for joy in our hobnail boots.

Then I climbed up high, away from all the leaping,
and I took off my boots and put them next to me.
I looked at the brightness, shining in the distance.
I watched as the sun crept over me.

And when I saw the rainbow, shining in the distance,
I knew it was a present
- just for me!

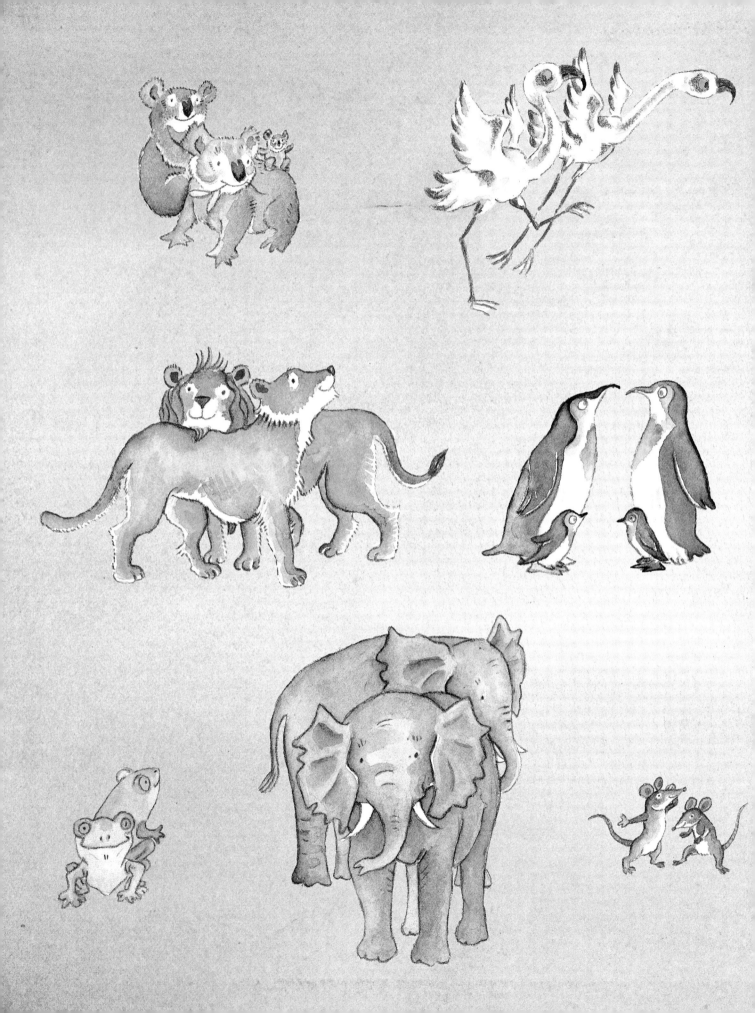